Dear Parent:
Your child's love of reading starts here!

Every child learns to read in a different way and at his or her own speed. Some go back and forth between reading levels and read favorite books again and again. Others read through each level in order. You can help your young reader improve and become more confident by encouraging his or her own interests and abilities. From books your child reads with you to the first books he or she reads alone, there are I Can Read Books for every stage of reading:

SHARED READING
Basic language, word repetition, and whimsical illustrations, ideal for sharing with your emergent reader

BEGINNING READING
Short sentences, familiar words, and simple concepts for children eager to read on their own

READING WITH HELP
Engaging stories, longer sentences, and language play for developing readers

READING ALONE
Complex plots, challenging vocabulary, and high-interest topics for the independent reader

ADVANCED READING
Short paragraphs, chapters, and exciting themes for the perfect bridge to chapter books

I Can Read Books have introduced children to the joy of reading since 1957. Featuring award-winning authors and illustrators and a fabulous cast of beloved characters, I Can Read Books set the standard for beginning readers.

A lifetime of discovery begins with the magical words "I Can Read!"

D1021552

/.icanread.com for information
; your child's reading experience.

TIME WARP TRIO

SOUTH POLE OR BUST (AN EGG)

Time Warp Trio created by Jon Scieszka

Adapted by Catherine Hapka

Based on the television script by Kathy Waugh

HarperCollins*Publishers*

Time Warp Trio™ is produced by WGBH in association with Soup2Nuts for Discovery Kids.
HarperCollins®, ☎®, and I Can Read Book® are trademarks of HarperCollins Publishers.

Library of Congress catalog card number: 2006935097
ISBN-10: 0-06-111641-6 (trade bdg.) — ISBN-13: 978-0-06-111641-4 (trade bdg.)
ISBN-10: 0-06-111640-8 (pbk.) — ISBN-13: 978-0-06-111640-7 (pbk.)

Typography by Joe Merkel
❖
First Edition

CONTENTS

Meet the Time Warp Trio:

Three ordinary boys
with an extraordinary book.

The Book

The Book looks like a book,

but acts like a time machine.

It's cool.

But there's one problem:

The only way to get back home

is to find *The Book* in

the new time.

And whenever the boys travel,

it has a habit of disappearing.

The Boys

Joe: An average kid. His uncle Joe gave him *The Book* for his birthday.

Sam: A smart kid. He tends to panic in scary situations.

Fred: A hungry kid. He doesn't always think before he acts.

CHAPTER 1
Snow Way

Three kids drop out of the sky
and into a snowbank.

"Hmm, snow," Joe says.

His friend Sam shivers.

"You forgot to mention the ice."

Fred smiles.

"Maybe it's a ski resort," he says.

"I hear voices."

"Yeah," Sam agrees.

"They're saying 'Fred is an idiot.'"

Joe, Sam, and Fred hike up

the nearest hill.

All they can see is icy water,

icy snow, and icy ice.

Suddenly the hill starts to shake.

"Was that an earthquake?" Sam asks.

"Maybe Fred just burped,"

Joe says.

CRA-A-A-A-ACK!

Their icy hill breaks loose

and floats out to sea. . . .

"We're doomed!" Sam yells.

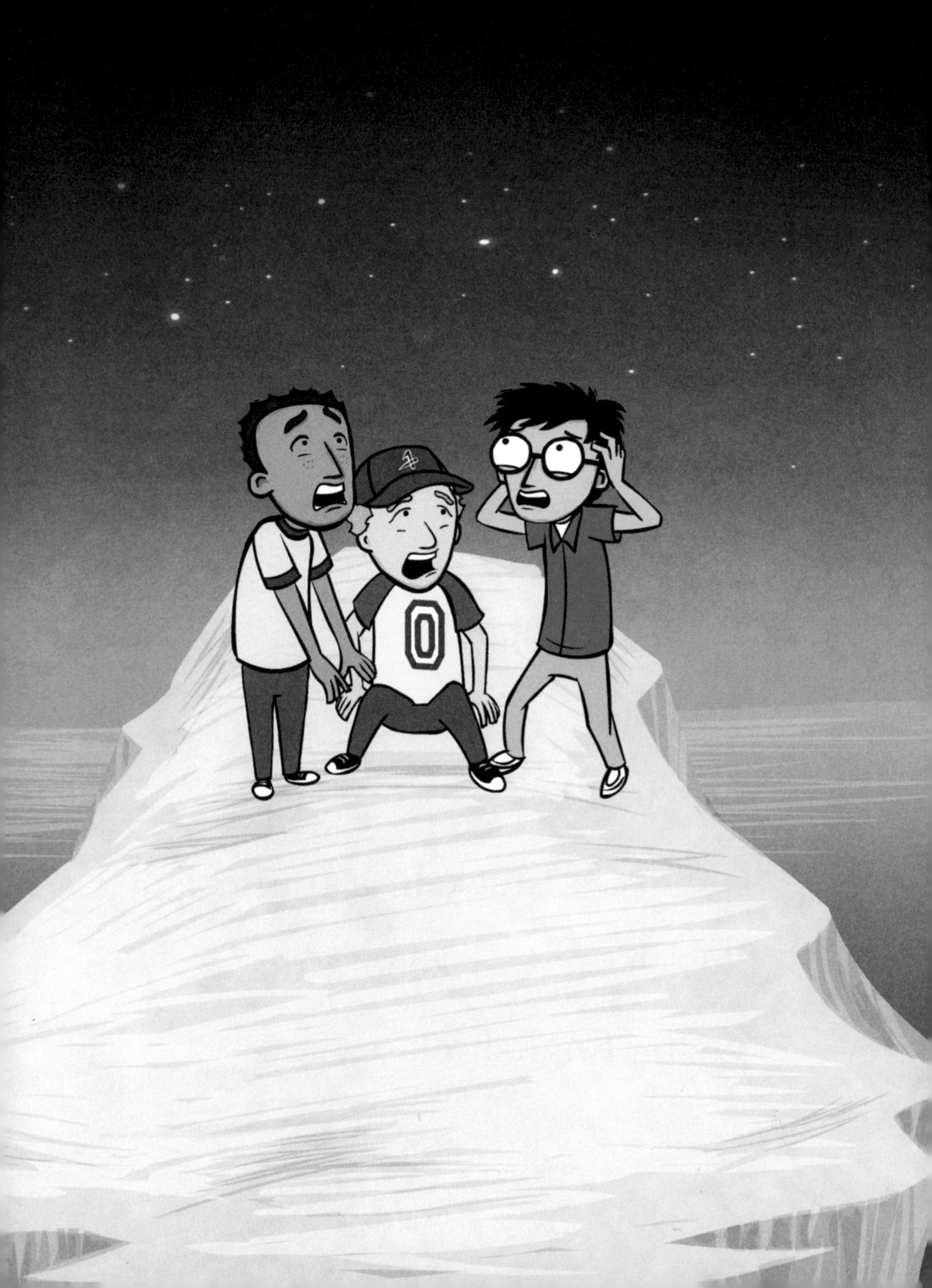

CHAPTER 2

A Few Minutes Earlier...

Joe's not happy.

It's hot.

He's cranky.

The car is stuck in a traffic jam.

Plus, he has to keep a diary

for his English class.

Then Fred has an idea.
"Let's use *The Book* and
go somewhere cooler."

Joe takes out *The Book*.

He tries to remember how it works.

Fred grabs it.

"Punch this button," he says.

"Then type in where you want to go."

Green mist pours out of *The Book*.

"Wait!" Fred cries.

"I didn't type anything yet . . ."

WHOOOOSH!

They fall out of the sky

and into a snowbank. . . .

CHAPTER 3

. . . And Now, Back to Our Story

Joe, Sam, and Fred shiver.

Even a hot car is better than this!

"Do you still have *The Book*?"

Sam asks Fred.

"I do," Joe says.

He pulls out a book—his diary.

"Sorry, wrong book."

Then they all hear a voice.

"Help is on the way, boys."

A man on shore tosses them a rope
and pulls them to safety.

"I'm Apsley Cherry-Garrard," he says.

He tells the boys where they are—
at the South Pole!

18

Cherry leads them back to his camp.
Along the way, the sun goes down.
Cherry tells them it won't be back
for six months.
"Here we are," Cherry says.
"Welcome to Cape Evans."

He leads the boys into a hut.
Several men are inside.
"Cherry!" one of the
men cries.
"Just in time for
your favorite meal."
The man's
name is
Birdie Bowers.
"Hello, laddies,"
Birdie says.
"Welcome to
Antarctica,"

20

The boys sit down.

"Wow . . . Antarctica," Sam says.

"And that calendar says 1911.
Could this be Scott's . . ."

Suddenly a strange smell

drifts through the hut.

Plop!

Birdie dumps something into

the boys' bowls.

Fred takes a bite.

"What is this?"

Another man looks up from his book.

"Hoosh," he answers.

"Dried meat, water, and seal's liver."

Fred takes another bite.

"Not bad."

CHAPTER 4
Great Scott!

"Who are you?"

Fred asks the man with the book.

"Captain Robert F. Scott,"

the man says.

"The leader of this expedition."

"Hey, I know you," says Fred.

"I saw your picture at

the Museum of Natural History."

"Of course you know me," Scott says. "All of England is waiting to hear that we've reached the South Pole." "Unless Amundsen beats us to it," Cherry adds.

The men were preparing
for the winter journey.
"Before heading to the Pole," Cherry
explains, "we're going to get the
eggs of the emperor penguin."
"If we can get the eggs,"
says a man named Wilson,
"we may be able to
find out if birds
evolved from reptiles."

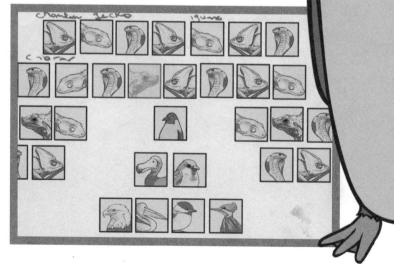

"Oh." Fred rolls his eyes.

"That explains it."

"It's simple," Wilson says.

"We'll haul our sleds
and climb down 800-foot cliffs to the
penguin nesting grounds."

"We'll work in the pitch dark,"
Cherry says, "in the coldest weather
imaginable!"

"We'll eat hoosh every night!"
Birdie cries.

"And wear the same smelly
underwear for weeks."

"What say you, boys?" the men ask.

"Ready to march into history?"

The boys all answer at once: "No!"

CHAPTER 5
Cold Eggs and Sam

That night Joe has an odd dream.

He is back in the hot car.

The car speaks to him.

"Are you looking for a book?"

"Yes!" the dreaming Joe cries.

"Then get out," the car voice says.

"And follow the penguin."

"That makes no sense," Joe says.

"This is a dream," the car answers.

"It's not supposed to make sense."

Joe climbs out and finds a penguin.

It's sitting on *The Book*!

Joe wakes up with a start.

"I know where *The Book* is," he says.

"We're going on the winter journey."

Sam and Fred aren't happy about this.

But soon they are hiking

over snowy

hills.

When night falls, they pitch a tent.

"It's chilly, laddies," Birdie says.

"It's 47 degrees below zero."

Joe writes in his diary:

"At 47 below, your teeth freeze."

It takes three weeks to reach

the penguin nesting grounds.

The boys look under

every penguin in sight.

But they can't find *The Book*.

Then things get worse.

"We're almost out of

food," Birdie says.

34

"Are you sure?" Cherry asks.

He shakes a food bag.

Something tumbles out.

Joe gasps. "*The Book*!"

CHAPTER 6
Mad About *The Book*

But when Joe hits the button
on *The Book*, nothing happens.
The keypad is frozen solid.
The boys try to thaw out *The Book*
by holding it over the fire.
But it's slow going.

That night, Joe hears a voice
calling him.

He crawls outside and gasps.

"Mad Jack! What are you

doing here?"

Mad Jack is the boys' enemy.

He wants to be the ruler

of all space and time.

"I'm here to see you," Mad Jack says.

"I brought you here.

This is the only place so cold

that *The Book* will not work."

"Okay," says Joe. "Now what?"

"I'll give you food," Mad Jack says,

"in exchange for *The Book.*"

Joe hesitates.

If he gives up *The Book*,

they will be stuck

in Antarctica forever.

But if he doesn't, they'll starve.

Joe walks back inside the tent.

Soon he returns.

"At last!" Mad Jack cries.

He sees *The Book*.

He's dreamed of owning it

his whole life.

He grabs it and runs away.

CHAPTER 7
Book or No Book

"I didn't have a choice,"

Joe says.

"Dinner!" Cherry calls.

"All the hoosh you can eat!"

"Yum," Sam mutters,

making a disgusted face.

Joe smiles.

"Want some pizza instead?"

Joe reaches under his pillow. . .

and pulls out *The Book*!

"Ah, finally," he says.

"It's completely thawed."

"But . . . you said . . ." Sam sputters.

Joe punches some buttons.

The Book glows.

Whoooosh!

The boys are back in the hot car.

"I gave Mad Jack a book," Joe explains.

"I didn't say *which* book."

In some other place and time, Mad Jack opens his new book.

"Dear diary," he reads aloud.

"Today sort of stinks. Joe."

THE END

THE COLD, HARD FACTS

First, the good news: Captain Robert Scott was one of the first men to ever reach the South Pole. The bad news: A Norwegian explorer named Roald Amundsen got there before him. The worst news: Scott never made it back alive.

What went wrong? Many people believe his trip was a disaster because he didn't use sled dogs—he made his men haul their own sleds most of the way. Not only that, Scott had a team of five explorers, and he barely brought enough food for four. Poor planning left Scott's team hungry and exhausted. He also let two of his best explorers, Birdie Bowers and Edward Wilson, go on a dangerous hunt for penguin eggs right before their journey to the South Pole. They thought the eggs might prove that birds descended from reptiles, but the eggs turned out to be scientifically worthless. (Talk about rotten eggs!) This journey left them weak and weary before their South Pole trek.

Captain Scott and his team did make it into the history books—unfortunately, not the way they had planned.